Geronimo Stilton™ Reporter

PAPERCUTZ™

Graphic Novels Available From Papercutz™

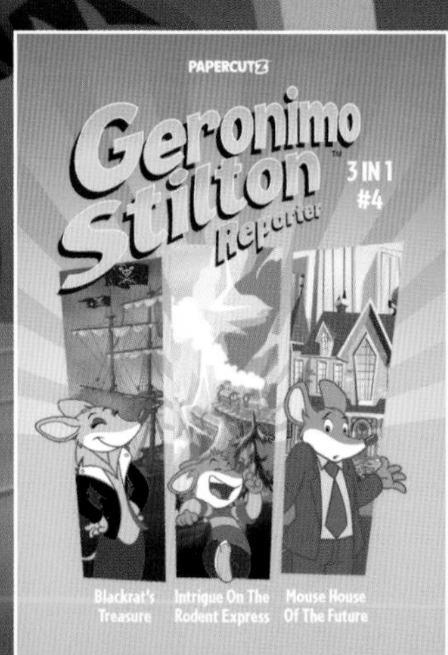

PAPERCUTZ

@papercutzgn / papercutz.com

Geronimo Stilton™ Reporter

#15 CLEAN SWEEP
By Geronimo Stilton

PAPERCUTZ™

CLEAN SWEEP

Text by GERONIMO STILTON
Cover by ALESSANDRO MUSCILLO (artist) and CHRISTIAN ALIPRANDI (colorist)
Editorial supervision by ALESSANDRA BERELLO (Atlantyca S.p.A.)
Editing by ANITA DENTI and ALICE GUALANDRIS (Atlantyca S.p.A.)
Script by DAVIDE COSTA
Art by ALESSANDRO MUSCILLO
Color by CHRISTIAN ALIPRANDI
Original Lettering by MARIA LETIZIA MIRABELLA

Special thanks to CARMEN CASTILLO

www.papercutz.com

Based on an original idea by Elisabetta Dami.

Based on the episode 15 of the Geronimo Stilton animated series *"Che fine ha fatto Tea,"* ("Clean Sweep")
written by ERIC SHAW, storyboard by DAVIDE VECA
Preview based on the episode 16 of the Geronimo Stilton animated series *"Che pasticcio, l'amore!,"* ("Mr. and Mrs. Matched")
written by CARIN GREENBERG BAKER, storyboard by RICCARDO AUDISIO

www.geronimostilton.com

JAYJAY JACKSON — Production
MIGUEL ZAPATA — Cover Design
WILSON RAMOS JR. — Lettering
STEPHANIE BROOKS — Editor
MIKE MARTS — Editor-in-Chief

ISBN: 978-1-5458-1135-1

Papercutz was founded by Terry Nantier and Jim Salicrup.

Printed in China
December 2023

First Printing

FRUSH
FRUSH

GAH!

SDLENG

CRICK
AAACK! HMM...

WHAT A DAY I'VE HAD...

I'M READY FOR SOME PEACE AND QUIET.
PLOP

PTEW
PTEW
GAH!
FWASH
SWOM

HEY, **UNCLE G**, YOU'RE JUST IN TIME FOR "MICE SQUAD ON THE MOON"!
OH... *UH.* CHEDDARRIFIC, **BEN!**

WOW, THIS IS THE ONE WHERE **MOON MOUSE** AND **NOVA** ESCAPE FROM THE CRATER MONSTER!
COULDN'T YOU WATCH SOMETHING A LITTLE MORE... QUIET?

OH, NO! NOT A SPECIAL NEWS REPORT. I'M GONNA MISS MY SHOW!
*THIS JUST IN... **NEW MOUSE CITY** HAS BECOME VICTIM TO A STRING OF LAWLESS AND FELONIOUS UNARMED INTRUSIONS AND THEFTS.*

I REPEAT, A RASH OF HEISTS HAVE STRUCK A NUMBER OF HIGH-END SHOPS IN THE **TRIPLE-CREAM SHOPPING DISTRICT.**

OH! THIS COULD BE A BIG STORY. BETTER HEAD BACK TO THE OFFICE IN CASE THERE ARE ANY CALLS.

COOL. I CAN CATCH THE REST OF THE MOUSE SQUAD ONLINE THERE, TOO!
-SIGH-... GREAT.

MOLDY MOZZARELLA! EIGHT STORES HAVE BEEN ROBBED...

...A JEWELRY STORE, CLOTHING STORE, LADIES' ACCESSORY STORE, AND A SHOE STORE. WHAT'S NEXT?

SLAM
GERONIMO! THEA HAS DISAPPEARED!

WHAAAT?!

I CAN'T BELIEVE SHE'S GONE. WHERE COULD SHE BE? WHERE COULD SHE GO?!
TRAP, CALM DOWN AND TELL US WHAT HAPPENED. FROM THE BEGINNING.

BOO HOO HOO... IT WAS TONIGHT. THEA WAS SUPPOSED TO MEET ME FOR DINNER AT ***THE CHEESE SHED*** AND--

--AND THEN--

--SHE ***NEVER*** SHOWED UP!

AND...?
AND WHAT? SHE NEVER SHOWED UP! THAT'S IT.

IS THAT ALL? THEA'S NOT ***MISSING.*** SHE HAD AN INTERVIEW TO DO AND PROBABLY LOST TRACK OF TIME AND FORGOT TO CANCEL YOUR DINNER.

BUT I TRIED TO CALL HER. AND I GOT HER VOICEMAIL!

HER *VOICEMAIL!*
STAY CALM! SHE'LL PROBABLY CALL YOU ANY MINUTE AND EXPLAIN WHAT HAPPENED.

REALLY? *HMMM*... I GUESS YOU'RE RIGHT?
SEE?

EVERYTHING HAS A REASONABLE EXPLANATION.

YEAH, GET HIM! LOOK OUT--ALIENS!

WELL. MOST EVERYTHING HAS A REASONABLE EXPLANATION.
UH, WHAT?

AH, ASIDE FROM ALL THE CRIMES TAKING PLACE IN ONE AREA OF THE CITY, THERE APPEARS TO BE NO CONNECTION BETWEEN ANY OF THEM.

HEY... I THINK I SEE A PATTERN...
REALLY?

THIS COULD BE THE BIG BREAK WE'RE LOOKING FOR. A-HA!
BUT WHAT...?

HUH?!
YOU SEE?

IT'S A SMILEY FACE! AND THIS HAS TO BE THE WORK OF SOME DEVIOUS MASTERMIND...

...WHO'S PROBABLY CALLED THE SMIRK! OR CROOKED FACE! OR SLASHMOUTH, OR--
--TRAP.

THERE IS NO PATTERN.
LOOK!

ANOTHER ROBBERY HAS TAKEN PLACE IN NEW MOUSE CITY. THE FAMOUS **MOUSEY'S DEPARTMENT STORE** WAS ROBBED!
OH, I KNEW IT...

...THE LAST PIECE OF THE PUZZLE!
OOPS!

EVERYBODY, GET SOME REST. TOMORROW WE'LL CHECK OUT THE TRIPLE-CREAM DISTRICT.

UH, TRAP? I THINK THAT'S FOR LADIES.
REALLY? OH, WELL...

IT'S GOOD!
EXCUSE ME...

...DO YOU HAVE A LIST OF THE ITEMS THAT WERE STOLEN?
OF COURSE I DO! IT'S A TRAGIC SITUATION--THEY EVEN TOOK A BEAUTIFUL HAT ADORNED WITH FEATHERS!

WE HAVE TO SAVE THE OTHERS!
BUT, I--
AS YOU CAN SEE, JUDKINS ISN'T HANDLING THIS WELL, DETECTIVE.

--WHAT SURPRISED ME THE MOST, DETECTIVE, WAS THE MANNER IN WHICH EVERYTHING WAS STOLEN!
OH, I'M NOT A DETECTIVE, I'M A--

IT WAS ALL DONE IN A CLEAN, ORDERLY FASHION. THEY EVEN TIDIED UP THE STOCK ROOM.
CURIOUS!

THE ONLY THING THEY LEFT BEHIND WAS THIS CLEAN WHITE GLOVE.

AND THIS CAN OF DISINFECTANT!
HMMMM...

ONE DRESS, AN EVENING GOWN, YELLOW. ONE PAIR OF PINK OPENED-TOED BEACH SANDALS. ONE PAIR OF JEANS, BLUE, PRE-SHRUNK. AND THE FEATHERED HAT.
WAAAH! MY HAT!

THIS LIST REMINDS ME OF SOMETHING...

DON'T YOU JUST LOVE THEM?
YEAH. ARE YOU GOING TO GET THEM?

NAH. I'M JUST LOOKING.

WHAT DO YOU THINK?
VERY NICE! ARE YOU GOING TO GET IT?

NAH, I JUST WANTED TO TRY IT.

OH, I JUST LOVE THESE!

YES, YES. I UNDERSTAND.

SHE WON'T BE TAKING THEM.
HMPH!

YOU DON'T KNOW HOW TO ENJOY SHOPPING, DO YOU?
I GUESS NOT...

WAIT A CHEDDAR-PICKING-MINUTE! WHEN THEA AND I WERE SHOPPING, I NOTICED THERE WAS THIS RAT IN SUNGLASSES THAT WE KEPT RUNNING INTO.
THEY'RE CALLED SALES CLERKS?

IT WAS SOME MYSTERIOUS GUY WHO WAS AT EACH STORE THAT WAS ROBBED. HE MIGHT BE OUR CONNECTION!
HMMM, TOO BAD HE DIDN'T HAVE A NAMETAG.

WHY?
BECAUSE THEN WE'D KNOW HIS NAME!

LET'S THINK ABOUT HOW WE CAN FIND THEA!
AND, I REPEAT, THIS WILL ALL BE FINE.

WOW, WHAT A DREAM. BUT, WAIT...

...WHERE AM I?!

WELL. AT LEAST SOMEONE'S GOT GOOD TASTE!

HOW IS THE REST OF THIS PLACE?

LOCKED?!

I'M ***TRAPPED!***
THE BARS ARE THERE FOR YOUR PROTECTION.

YOU--PRINCE NOGOUDA?!
AND ALSO TO PREVENT YOU FROM LEAVING!

WELCOME, TO MY HUMBLE HOME. I AM HAPPY YOU COULD COME FOR ANOTHER VISIT.
VISIT?

YOU'RE HOLDING ME PRISONER!

WELL, IT'S BEEN REAL.
HOP

AH!

BUT I GOTTA GO!

OUCH!
WHUMP
NO, STOP!

YOU'RE SPREADING GERMS!

I **HATE** GERMS.
SPRITZ SPRITZ

AND I HATE TO BE A PRISONER!

GRAB
WOOSH

AH!
THUD

FREE!
...OR NOT!
YOINK

OOF!
WHUD

PERHAPS A LITTLE DINNER MIGHT IMPROVE YOUR MOOD, MY SOON-TO-BE PRINCESS.
A CANDLELIGHT DINNER FOR TWO, UNDER THE STARS. SEE YOU TONIGHT.
YOU AREN'T MY TYPE, RATTY!

DID HE SAY "PRINCESS"?!

THE STOLEN ITEMS INCLUDE DRESSES, JEWELS, SHOES, COOKWARE, JEANS AND ACCESSORIES.
DO YOU THINK THE SALES CLERK TOOK IT ALL?

HEY, UNC, I'VE BEEN CALLING THEA ALL MORNING AND STILL NO LUCK.

THAT'S WHAT I WAS SAYING, WASN'T IT?
NO REPLY? *HM*, THAT ***IS*** ODD...

TOLD YOU SHE'S MISSING. DISAPPEARED. VAMOOSED! JUST GONE!

HMMMM, MAYBE IF I CAN TRACK HER CREDIT CARDS, PASSPORT, OR DRIVER'S LICENSE...
...NOTHING!

ZIP, ZILCH, NADA! SHE'S JUST ***GOOOONE!***

HM. WELL, THEA'S A BIG GIRL AND SHE CAN HANDLE HERSELF. I'M SURE SHE'LL LET US KNOW IF SOMETHING'S WRONG.

OH! OH, NO! CHECK THIS--THEA NEVER SHOWED UP TO HER KARATE CLASS!

WHAT?! SHE ***NEVER*** MISSES HER KARATE CLASS. SOMETHING'S WRONG!

LET'S GO.

I ALMOST FORGOT!

HEHEHE. TIME TO MAKE A PHONE CALL...

TLAK

DONE. I NOTIFIED THE POLICE OF THEA'S DISAPPEARANCE... HUNH?

WHAT... I'M ON?

THIS JUST IN, FOLLOWING A RASH OF ROBBERIES THROUGHOUT NEW MOUSE CITY, ONE THEA STILTON WHO WORKS FOR **THE RODENT'S GAZETTE** HAS SUDDENLY GONE MISSING.

A COINCIDENCE?
OH, THAT IS JUST LIKE **SALLY** TO STIR THINGS UP!
SHE'S RIGHT ABOUT ONE THING. THE ROBBERIES AND THEA'S DISAPPEARANCE MIGHT BE CONNECTED.
CUZ, YOU DON'T THINK--?

YES! THAT MYSTERIOUS RAT MIGHT BE RESPONSIBLE FOR EVERYTHING.

WELL, AT LEAST SALLY'S STORY WON'T HURT BUSINESS.
RING

HELLO! RODENT'S GAZETTE. YES, MA'AM. OH, OOOKAY, YOU GOT IT.
TRAP, WHO WAS THAT?

SOME WOMAN JUST CANCELING HER SUBSCRIPTION TO THE GAZETTE.
WHAT? WHY?!

OH, BECAUSE THEA WAS IMPLICATED IN THE ROBBERIES.
RING

HELLO? RODENT'S GAZETTE. YES... BUT THEA IS NOT INVOLVED WITH THE ROBBERIES.

RODENT'S GAZETTE? NO, THEA IS NOT A CRIMINAL!

NO, THEA IS NOT A CRIMINAL!

IF THIS KEEPS UP, IT COULD BE THE END OF THE WHOLE STILTON COMPANY!

UUUUFFF!

-GNNN!-
THERE HAS TO BE A WAY OUT!

MMMH...

NOT FROM HERE.

PERHAPS THERE...?

OHHH...

...NEVER MIND.

HOW UNFORTUNATE.

MAYBE WITH THAT, I CAN CONNECT WITH BEN...
...NOW, LET'S SEE IF BENJAMIN IS ON HIS BENPAD.

HAHA. WHEN IS HE ***NOT*** ON HIS BENPAD?
12345678

TAP
TAP
TAP
TAP
TAP
12:54

BUT, MA'AM... BUT... OKAY, IF THAT'S THE WAY YOU WANT IT!

THAT WAS MY MOTHER, SHE JUST CANCELED HER SUBSCRIPTION.
-SIGH.-
BIP BEEP
BIP BIP

BEEP BEEP
BIP BIP
BIP BEEP
BEEP
HEY, THAT'S MORSE CODE... FROM THEA! SOUNDS LIKE DIRECTIONS?

IT LOOKS LIKE... THE BANDEL JUNGLE!
OF COURSE IT'S NOGOUDA!
BUT ISN'T HE IN JAIL?

ACCORDING TO THIS, HE WAS IN JAIL. BUT HE WAS LET OUT FOR CLEAN BEHAVIOR.

THERE ISN'T ENOUGH DISINFECTANT IN THE WORLD FOR A DIRTY CONSCIENCE. LET'S GO!

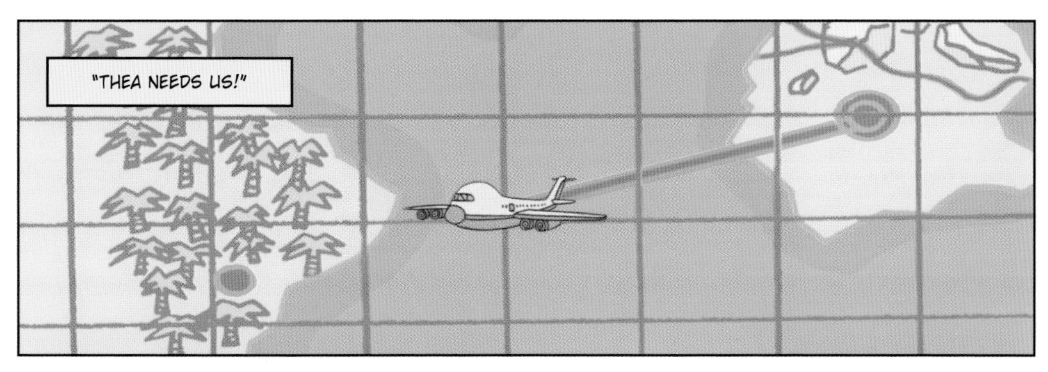
"THEA NEEDS US!"

I CAN'T BELIEVE THAT YOU WOULD STOOP SO LOW AS TO DRAG ME INTO THE JUNGLE TO BE YOUR PRINCESS!

WELL, YOU WEREN'T MY FIRST CHOICE.
WHAT?! HOW **DARE** YOU!

I CAN'T BELIEVE THAT YOU WOULD THINK SOMEONE ELSE COULD MAKE A BETTER PRINCESS THAN ME?
NOT THAT I WOULD EVER BE YOUR PRINCESS...

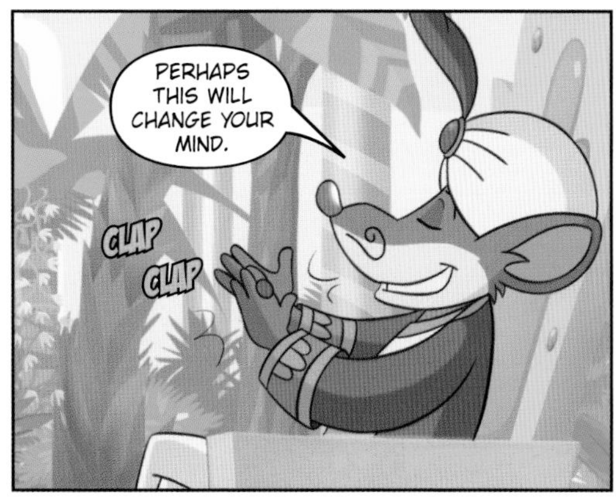
PERHAPS THIS WILL CHANGE YOUR MIND.
CLAP
CLAP

OHH! YOU STOLE THOSE ITEMS, B-BUT WHY...? YOU CAN BUY ANYTHING YOU WANT!
MEH...

YES, WELL, I'M A LITTLE BROKE AT THE MOMENT, AT LEAST UNTIL I FIND A PRINCESS.

SWEET! BUT, AH, NO THANKS.

HOLDING A GIRL AGAINST HER WILL IS A BIG TURN-OFF.
OH, YOU WILL DO WHAT I ASK... AND YOU'LL DO IT BEFORE TOMORROW COMES.

GUARDS!
HMPH!

YOU DON'T
HAVE A CHOICE.

THE STARS
ARE ALIGNING,
AND IT'S DESTINY,
MY PRINCESS.
GUARDS!
SNAP

BUT...

YOU...!

RAAAAAT!

AH! BUGS! BUGS! -›KOFF KOFF!‹-

-›ACK!‹- I THINK I SWALLOWED ONE.
OOOH, THAT'S NOT GOOD. NOW YOU'VE GOT ONE ON THE INSIDE.

AAAAHHHH!
ANOTHER MESSAGE FROM THEA. WE MUST BE CLOSE.

UFF. OKAY. I'M BETTER NOW. TO THEA.
SHE'S NEAR HERE!

THEA WAS VERY PRECISE WITH THE COORDINATES!

THERE HAS TO BE SOME WAY FOR US TO SNEAK INTO THE PALACE...?
SNIFF! SNIFF! WHAT IS THAT SMELL?

IT'S COMING FROM THERE! THAT'S OUR WAY IN.
ARGH!

YOU GO FIRST.
NO, YOU GO FIRST.
NO, ***YOU*** FIRST!
NO, ***YOU!***
YOU!

ARGH! FINE!

I'LL GO, BUT I WON'T LIKE IT...

I AM NOT HAPPY.
WE CAN'T SEE ANYTHING!

WHAT LUCK, I FOUND A LIGHT SWITCH!

BLUB!

HUH, THAT'S A WEIRD LIGHT SWITCH!
OKAY, NEW RULE--NOBODY TOUCHES ANYTHING! UNDERSTOOD?
UNDERSTOOD.

WHAT...

...IS...

...HAPPENING?!

FANTASTIC...

ACH!

GET AWAY, YOU BUFFOON. YOU GOT GERMS ON MY TELESCOPE!

AND I HATE GERMS!
SQUEAK
SQUEAK

THE MOON IS ASCENDING. THE STARS ARE ALIGNING... THE TIME IS NEAR.

ONCE I HAVE MY PRINCESS, I WILL BE PRINCE OF THE BANDEL JUNGLE! FOR ALL TIME!

AND EVERYTHING IS IN PLACE?
PREPARATIONS ARE BEING FINALIZED NOW.
IT'S GOING TO BE A FANTASTIC WEDDING!
S-STOP PUSHING, YOU BEASTS!

I'M GOING, I'M GOING!

WELCOME.

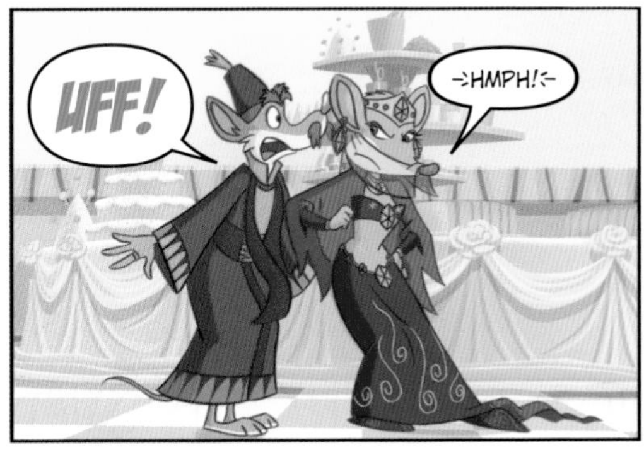
UFF!
-HMPH!-

I SERVE ALONE.

WELL, IT CERTAINLY IS CLEAN.

AND LEMON FRESH!
WELL, CLEANLINESS SEEMS TO BE CUSTOMARY HERE.
CUSTOM... CUSTOM... WHY, THAT'S IT--THE BANDEL CUSTOM! WHAT MONTH IS THIS?

I THINK IT'S WEDNESDAY?

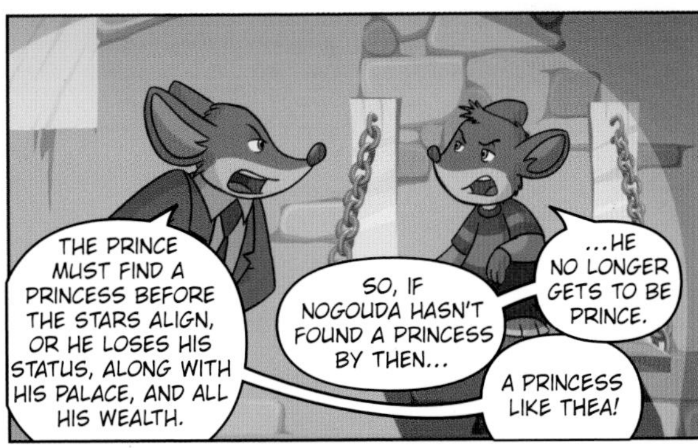
THE PRINCE MUST FIND A PRINCESS BEFORE THE STARS ALIGN, OR HE LOSES HIS STATUS, ALONG WITH HIS PALACE, AND ALL HIS WEALTH.
SO, IF NOGOUDA HASN'T FOUND A PRINCESS BY THEN...
...HE NO LONGER GETS TO BE PRINCE.
A PRINCESS LIKE THEA!

RIGHT! I THINK I KNOW HOW WE CAN GET OUT OF HERE. HUDDLE UP.

IS IT SAFE, CUZ?
OKAY!
YES. PUSH, BENJAMIN.

UHHH... GUYS, WE HAVE A LITTLE PROBLEM...

THERE'S AN ALLIGATOR GUARD OUTSIDE!

PULL, BEN!
I'M *PULLING*, UNCLE G!
SNAP
AAH!

WOW, THAT WAS CLOSE!

THIS FRIGHT...

...GOT ME HUNGRY!

GOOD THING I ALWAYS PACK AN EMERGENCY SANDWICH...
...HEY!
I HAVE AN IDEA!

A GOOD KNOT...

...AND LET'S GO FISHING.

HOPE IT BITES!
SMACK

CLANK

BE CAREFUL!

GET READY TO RUN...

...NOW!

CHOMP

LET'S GO LOOK FOR THEA!

HURRY UP, MY BEAUTIFUL PRINCESS.
I AM NOT A PRINCESS!
NOT YET!

YOU FORGOT TO INVITE SOME GUESTS.

GUARDS, SEIZE THEM AT ONCE!

WAIT, YOU FORGOT SOMETHING. ACCORDING TO ANCIENT BANDEL LAW, THE PRINCE IS NOT ALLOWED TO TAKE A PRINCESS WITHOUT WEARING THE SACRED FAMILY MEDALLION.

REALLY?! EVERYONE, STAY PUT, I'LL HAVE TO CHECK THE BANDEL BOOK OF CUSTOMS.

I'LL BE RIGHT BACK.

IT'S A PITY TO WASTE ALL THAT FOOD, ISN'T IT?

IT IS A PITY TO WASTE ALL THAT FOOD, ISN'T IT?
WINK

AH!

AH!

BAM

THUD
OH, YES!

FWISH

A SNACK? THANK YOU!
DON'T EAT IT, **USE** IT!

CRACK

MMMFFF!

EVERYONE, TOGETHER!

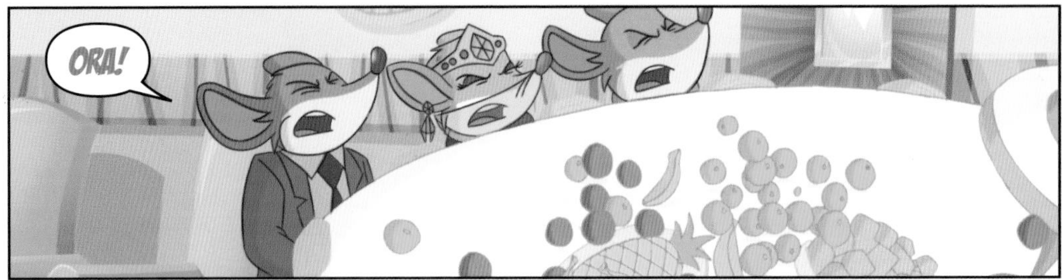
ORA!

ARGH!

NO!
UUFF!

GOOD JOB, TEAM. NOW LET'S SAY HI TO NOGOUDA!

UH... *AH*, OKAY. DUH-DUH-DUH-DUH-DUH... PRINCE MUST MAINTAIN HIS SHAPELY FIGURE... PRINCE MUST FLOSS...
...HERE IT IS. *UH*, THERE'S NO RULE ABOUT MEDALLIONS?

HE TRICKED ME!
GUAAAAAAARDS!

HOW DID YOU KNOW ABOUT THE MEDALLION?
I MADE IT UP. NOGOUDA IS SUCH A STICKLER FOR RULES, I FIGURED HE'D HAVE TO CHECK TO MAKE SURE.
HUH! SO, YOU BLUFFED HIM? WAY TO GO, UNC!

TRAP, WHY DON'T YOU TURN ON THE LIGHTS?

OH, NO, THAT'S A WEIRD LIGHT.

OH, WAIT... I GET IT!

SPLASH

RRRRUMBLE

BAM

GURGLE

WE DID IT! AND THERE'S NO MOSQUITOS NOW.

GREAT... NOW I'M NO LONGER THE PRINCE!

IT'S TOO LATE.

AND THE STARS ARE NO LONGER ALIGNED. WHAT COULD BE WORSE?!

OH, NO! AN ALLIGATOR!

NOOOOOO!

THUS PROVING THAT THE EVIL CRIMINAL BEHIND NEW MOUSE CITY'S RECENT RASH OF BURGLARIES WAS NONE OTHER THAN...

...THE **FORMER** PRINCE NOGOUDA!

AND **NOT** ONE THEA STILTON, AS WAS REPORTED BY THE DAILY RAT.

FOR THE RODENT'S GAZETTE, I'M GERONIMO STILTON.
HMPF!

VERY ELEGANT, STILTON.

HMPF!

RING

DAILY RAT, HOW MAY I HELP YOU ?
WHAT?!

NOBODY CANCELS ON ME!

AND NOW A SNEAK PREVIEW FROM THE NEXT BOOK IN GERONIMO'S SERIES...

PAPERCUTZ

Geronimo Stilton Reporter

MR. AND MRS. MATCHED

OH, WHAT A BEAUTIFUL DAY.
SIX HAPPY DAYS ON A CRUISE!
COME ON, JOIN ME IN THE POOL. IT'S HOT OUT!
IN A LITTLE BIT, THEY'LL SERVE LUNCH.
DID YOU ORDER ME A DRINK?

YOUR BEVERAGE, SIR!
OH-HO! MUCH OBLIGED.

VRRROOOM

HOW IS EVERYTHING OVER HERE?

VRRROOOM

VRRROOOM

BOING

THIS IS A STICK-UP! HAND OVER YOUR VALUABLES!
OH, NO. MY MONEY!
I'M AFRAID!

HMM?

BUT, THAT'S...

HOLD ON.
HERE YOU ARE...
TAKE IT!
HERE YOU GO. WHAT BAD LUCK...

HUM?

OVER MY DEAD BODY, YOU HEAR ME?!

OKAY.
UHH...

AS I SUSPECTED!

OH, NO...

...MY HAIR!

HEH HEH. NICE DOING BUSINESS WITH YA.

SEE YOU NEXT TIME!

HOP

SOMEONE CALL THE POLICE!

VRRROOOM

DARN YOU!

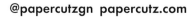

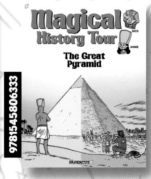

9781545806340
Magical History Tour
NICO
ANNIE
The Great Wall of China
PAPERCUTZ

9781545808948
FABRICE ERRE • SYLVAIN SAVOIA
Magical History Tour
NICO
ANNIE
The First Steps on the Moon
PAPERCUTZ

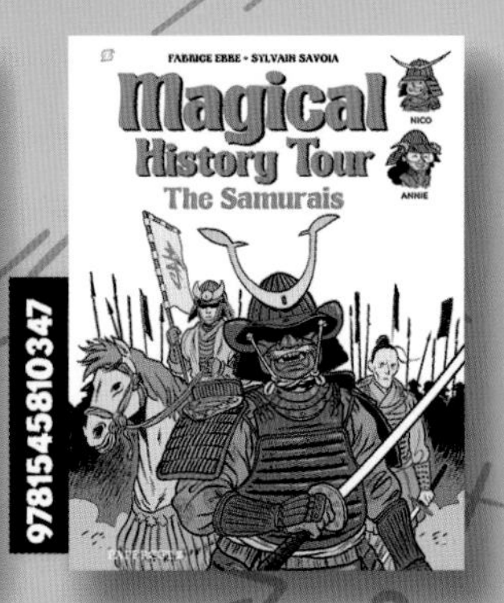
9781545810347
FABRICE ERRE • SYLVAIN SAVOIA
Magical History Tour
The Samurais
NICO
ANNIE

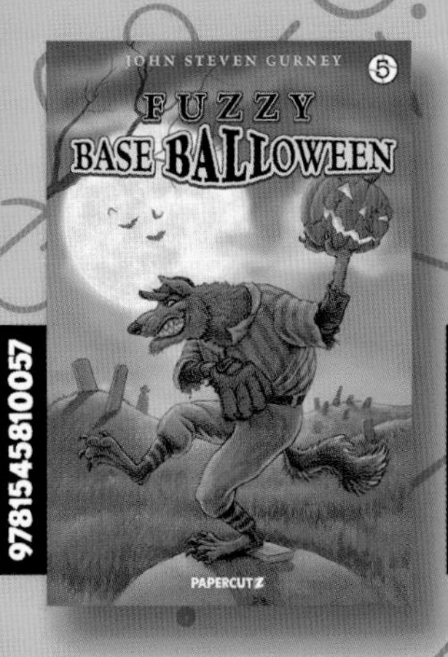
9781545810057
JOHN STEVEN GURNEY
5
FUZZY BASEBALLOWEEN
PAPERCUTZ

9781545807217
RACHAEL SMITH
BENJAMIN DICKSON
the Queen's favorite Witch
PAPERCUTZ

9781545809839
RACHAEL SMITH
BENJAMIN DICKSON
the Queen's favorite Witch
THE WHEEL OF FORTUNE
PAPERCUTZ

9781545810217
FERMIN SOLÍS
ASTRO MOUSE AND LIGHT BULB
Return to an Unknown Earth
PAPERCUTZ

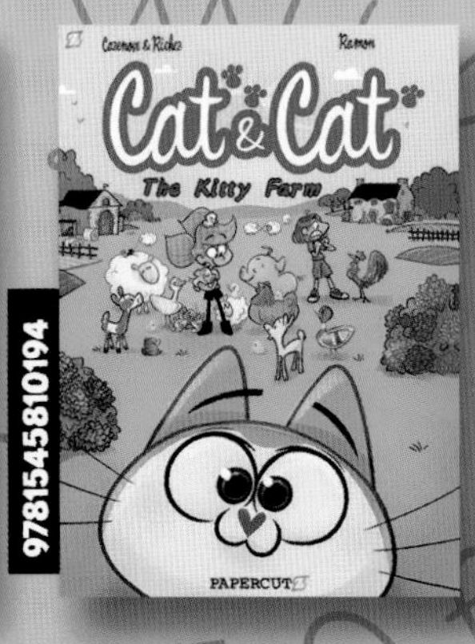
9781545810194
Cazenove & Richez
Ramon
Cat & Cat
The Kitty Farm
PAPERCUTZ

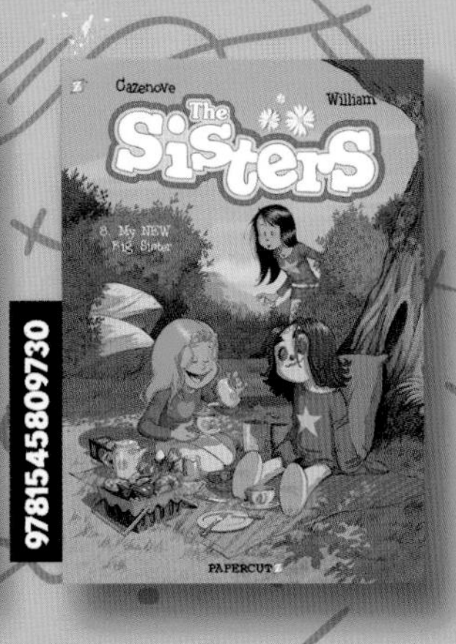
9781545809730
Cazenove
William
The Sisters
PAPERCUTZ